To

Carol Lynn Pearson

Morning Glory Mother

St. Martin's Press
New York

Design by Maureen Troy

ISBN 0-312-15592-1

First Edition: May 1997

10 9 8 7 6 5 4 3 2 1

To Jennifer Enderlin
who planted the seeds for
Morning Glory Mother

Morning Glory Mother

*Chapter
One*

IT IS PROBABLE THAT ALISON WOULD NOT have even considered running away from home on Mother's Day if three straws had not within a very short period of time fallen on the camel's back of her eternal maternal devotion.

The first one fell Saturday morning at three A.M. She had gone to bed early the night before, very tired after a week of teaching third-graders at Valley View Elementary.

"Just testing your eyesight, Jamie," she said, pointing to the little plastic sign above the sink. "Read."

Fourteen-year-old Jamie adopted his insolent

humor-the-mother voice and read in singsong, " 'This is a self-cleaning kitchen—clean it yourself.' "

"Don't get smart with me, Cookie," Alison said, giving her son a poke in the ribs. "I want this place to shine. I get very depressed when I walk into a kitchen that looks like a pigsty. And when I get depressed, I can either—one, go to bed for a week, or, two, buy myself a new condo on Waikiki Beach. And since this month I can't afford a new condo on Waikiki Beach, *nor* can I afford to go to bed for a week, I need to have you clean up the kitchen. Got it?"

"Sure, Mom," said Jamie, hauling out more graham crackers and milk for himself and the two friends in the other room playing video games. Their banana peels and the makings for pizza already covered the counters. "But give your speech to jerk-face there. She's the one who leaves everything out."

"Do not!"

"Okay, Melissa." Alison turned to her daughter, who was hauling out the butter and sugar. "About those cookies you're starting. You are not exempt from cleanup. I don't care what Mister Rogers says, you are not *that* special. I don't want to find one shred of evidence when I get up in the morning. Do you understand? Not one measuring spoon. Not one floury fingerprint. Got it?"

"Okay, okay, okay, okay," replied Melissa, as she threw a chocolate chip in the air and caught it in her mouth like a fish catches a fly. Melissa was eleven and suddenly nearly as tall as her mother, with the same hazel-green eyes and dark blond hair, only Alison's was short and permed and Melissa's long and straight.

Jamie, dark like his father, was even taller than his mother, a fact that made it all the more difficult for Alison to preside with authority. When your kids are shorter than you, you can look down and say, "Hey, the radio goes off now." But once you look up, you find yourself saying things like, "Jamie, could you turn down the radio—please?" Life turns into a whole different ball game when your kids are taller than you.

Especially if you're a divorced single mother.

When Alison got up at three to make a bathroom visit, she saw that the kitchen light was still on and went in to turn it off. Darn kids, don't ever think about the electric bill. She took one look and groaned. Everything was exactly as she had last seen it—*plus* a mountain of pans in the sink, *plus* dried cookie batter on the counter and drips on the floor, *plus* cracker crumbs and milk glasses and pizza crusts *and three-quarters of a gallon of milk* just sitting there; good, expensive two-percent milk bought with her carefully budgeted grocery money—just sitting there souring before her bleary eyes.

Alison sighed and sat herself down on a kitchen chair and stared. Then her eyes traveled to a little plastic sign she had posted on the refrigerator: "Help me to serve without thought of recognition—Anonymous." Yup.

And above it: "I bake, therefore I am—Mrs. Descartes."

No question, Alison thought. I clean the kitchen, therefore I am. I mop, therefore I am. I pick up after my children, therefore I am.

Resentment turned on like a faucet and flooded through her. What I really ought to do, she thought, is go get them, just get them up right now in the middle of the night and make them clean up this mess. No, they need their sleep—I thought I heard a bit of a cold in Melissa's voice last night. First thing in the morning when they get up . . . Or am I always too easy on them? No. . . .

Her eye caught the little sign on the cupboard door: ''The key to flexibility is indecision.''

She hit the table with her fist, spreading something sticky. ''That's it,'' she said out loud. ''I'm too darn flexible. I'm a pushover. I'm a doormat.''

Before she could reconsider, Alison stomped to the fireplace and picked up the old cowbell that sat on the hearth along with an antique iron and butter churn, the cowbell that she let the kids keep by their beds when they were sick. Well, this time *she* was sick, sick of being the only one in the house who seemed to care, sick of being the mother who nobody listened to or appreciated.

Holding the clangor, she strode down the hall, threw open Jamie's door, turned on the light, and stood by his bed. He looked so peaceful, so innocent with his mouth slightly open. Alison used to sneak into his room sometimes after he'd gone to bed and just look, just watch the sweet miracle of a child sleeping. Now she gently lifted the blanket that was down around his waist and brought it up to tuck around his chin.

Then she rang the cowbell.

"Up! Up! Up, up, up!" she shouted. "Time to get up! Time to get up and clean the kitchen!"

Jamie jackknifed to a sitting position, his eyes still closed. "What?"

Quickly crossing the hall, Alison threw open Melissa's door and rang the bell inches from her head. "Up! Up, I tell you! Up and clean the kitchen!"

Melissa rolled over and opened one shocked eye. "Mo-om! In the morning."

Standing in the hallway with a view of both her blinking children, Alison continued ringing the cowbell and yelling over the loud metallic sound. "I will not have it! Into the self-cleaning kitchen right now—both of you! *And not one word!*"

First Melissa, then Jamie stumbled out of bed.

That was the first straw.

Chapter Two

THE SECOND STRAW FELL ABOUT NOON OF the same Saturday. When Alison answered the door-bell, there stood Anne and John, the older two of the four Harris children from next door, holding a pink cut-glass plate carefully covered with Saran wrap.

"Hi, Mrs. Andrews. How are you?" Anne smiled warmly.

"Well, fine, thanks. How about yourself?"

"Just great!"

"We have a favor to ask." John indicated the plate his sister was holding. "We made crêpes with vanilla pudding and strawberries for Mom's breakfast in bed tomorrow morning—Mother's Day, you know.''

''But it's a surprise,'' Anne broke in eagerly. ''So we thought—could we please hide them in your refrigerator until morning?''

''Well, of course.'' Alison reached for the plate.

''Gee, thanks,'' said John. ''Dad's going to be out of town tomorrow on a business trip, so a special day for Mom is all up to us.''

''She's Mother of the Year at the church program tomorrow, you know,'' added Anne proudly.

''Yes, I know.''

''Well, gotta run. Mom will be back soon from teaching her aerobics class. We're planting another rosebush out by her bedroom window. This is the sixteenth—one for every year she's been a mother. See you tomorrow.''

''See you.''

''And thanks a lot!''

Alison watched the two Harris children run back to their two-story white house with its perfectly trimmed lawn and carefully tended colorful beds of pansies and petunias and azaleas.

Putting the pink plate in the refrigerator beside the leftover stew in the cottage cheese container, Alison lifted the Saran wrap and pinched off the teeniest fraction of an inch from one of the beautifully browned and rolled crêpes. Mmmmm. Delicious.

Then she stepped outside and watched the two Harris children run laughing into their backyard. She bent down and pulled a few of the taller weeds from her own little flower bed. No roses here. Plenty of morning glory, though, some that she had planted and some that seemed to grow from nowhere. Morning glory was pretty in its pinks and whites and blues, but it sure wasn't roses. Roses were classy—like Martha. Morning glory was common—like Alison.

Alison had often thought there should be better zoning laws. Imperfect families should not be allowed to live next door to perfect families, that's all there was to it. Every one of her own innumerable flaws was magnified in the contrast between Alison Andrews and Martha Harris.

If only Martha were a phony, a hypocrite, just pretending to be perfect. But Alison had long since acknowledged that Martha was sincerely and truly a wonderful person, charming, generous to all, efficient, and—no question about it—a perfect mother.

That hurt the most. A perfect mother. If Alison were that good a mother, Jamie and Melissa would serve her breakfast in bed and plant rosebushes for her. It wasn't *their* fault they were inconsiderate—it was *her* fault.

If she were a better person, so much would be different. Her children would have a father and that awful confusing divorce would never have taken place. She couldn't think just how, but surely it was ultimately her fault.

Oh, she had gone into the business of making a family with such enthusiasm. She was going to be the perfect wife and the perfect mother and the perfect teacher. She had visions of herself dancing through her days, feather duster in one hand and lesson plans in the other, then just for exercise bicycling to the grocery store with one or two wagons tied on behind, in which the children sat contentedly eating small boxes of raisins. And then having enough energy left over at the end of a full, full day to greet her husband seductively at the door wearing Saran wrap. But soon she was too tired even to *find* her bicycle, and had forgotten even how to *spell* "seductive."

What happened? She never quite knew, but certainly it was ultimately her fault—her fault that her energy gave out before the things on her list did; her fault that she resented working as hard as her husband did from eight to five and then having to do almost everything at home between five and eleven; her fault that she and Gary began to fight and criticize each other; her fault that he found somebody else; her fault that she was now alone and on overload all the time, knowing that the next shift is never coming in.

For the last five years on Valentine's Day the cupids and arrows she helped the children in her classroom make broke her heart all over again. If she'd been a better wife, prettier, softer, stronger, more mature, more childlike, more confident, more dependent—

more everything—she would have been more loveable and Gary would have loved her more and he would never have left.

And then she barely got over the guilt of Valentine's Day when she was hit with the guilt of Mother's Day.

If she were a better mother, her children would not be fatherless, and they would be thriving in some ways that they now seemed to be stuck.

If she were a better mother, her car would sport a bumper sticker that said, ''Proud parent of an honor student at Midvale Junior High,'' like Martha Harris' car did. Martha's car had *four* stickers like that. *And* it was always clean!

If she were a better mother, strains of early-morning Suzuki practice on the piano and the violin would come wafting like the smell of homemade bread from her house like they came wafting from the Harris house.

If she were a better mother, her banana bread would not have a crack down the middle and she would even bring to PTA events fruit pies with strips of dough braided deftly across the top like Martha Harris did.

If she were a better mother, she would not have

responded to Jamie's complaint that he was sick of those little round slice-and-bake cookies by cutting them on the diagonal.

And her children would win science prizes and citizenship prizes and Eagle Scout awards. And they would not fight at the table if their elbows happened to touch.

If she were a better mother, she would never have had to apologize to the Sears people for little Jamie not knowing the bathroom set was only for display.

And she would be able to take her children to Scotland for the summer instead of slowly saving up for a trip to Disneyland.

And she would have known that the cars for the Cub Scout pinewood derby needed to have their wheels sanded *before* you put graphite on them.

And Melissa would not be developing a weight problem at age eleven. And Jamie would never, never have gotten into trouble at school because he scratched a bad word on the principal's door.

If only Alison were a better mother, so many things would be different. But mostly—oh, mostly—they would show her a little appreciation from time to time.

They would even say "I love you" first instead of mumbling "You too." She loved her children dearly, and she could list many good qualities of each. She would not trade them for anything, even for the perfect Harris children.

But if only she were a better mother, a Rose Mother instead of a Morning Glory Mother, somebody would serve her breakfast in bed on Mother's Day, perhaps even thin crêpes with vanilla pudding and strawberries. Seeing so clearly her own inadequacies as she watched the Harris children enthusiastically plant the sixteenth rosebush outside their mother's bedroom window— that was the second straw.

Alison sighed. Mother of the Year. Of course Martha Harris was chosen to be the representative mother to be honored tomorrow in the Mother's Day program at church. The minister had decided that motherhood was not being given its due in this age in which women could climb the corporate ladder just like men, so a special committee of fathers had come up with a Mother's Day program to beat all Mother's Day programs. All the kids were to participate and Martha was to give a "response."

Speaking of which, it was nearly time for her to pick up her kids from swimming and take them over to the church to rehearse the Mother's Day program. Alison grabbed her keys and headed out the kitchen door.

And there, at the church, is where the third— and final—straw fell.

Chapter Three

AS SOON AS ALISON WALKED INTO THE HALL
where the program was to be, her mouth fell open.
Whoa! The men were really doing a job on this
Mother's Day thing. The stage was decorated with a
large backdrop on which a golden crown had been
painted, and above it the glittering words "Queen of
Our Home." In the center was an elevated throne,
which two men were busily covering with purple velvet, old drapes that Alison recognized from the elementary school auditorium.

Oh, brother, thought Alison as she surveyed the
scene. Who came up with this bright idea? Queen

of Our Home? Who were they talking about? Certainly not her. It takes more than one day of glitter and words to make a mother feel like Queen of Our Home. What Alison was feeling right now was— yes, one more layer of guilt. If she were a better mother, the children would treat her three-hundred and sixty-five days out of the year as Queen of Our Home.

"Hey, Alison!" Tom Howard stood back from the throne with his staple gun in hand. "How does that look?"

"Great!" Alison walked to the front of the hall. "You guys are doing some major production here."

"Nothing's too good for the Queens of Our Homes." He said it without sarcasm.

Alison smiled. At least the men were doing all the work on this program. They were even baking the treats and making the punch, and each man had been told he *had* to do it all *himself*. Alison's mother had told her of a Mother's Day for which the *women* had been asked to make the little carnation corsages that were passed out to them by the smiling children at the end of the Sunday service. Well, she thought, progress has been made. Nobody had called her to help paint the golden crown.

"Martha!" Tom called. "Could you come out here a minute?"

Martha Harris emerged from stage left, queenly even without the throne, flowing in a white pantsuit and heels, accented with a violet silk scarf. Her shining brunette hair was cut shoulder length and turned slightly under. Alison thought she could even smell Martha's perfume, gardenia.

"Let me show you how to step up on this deal without falling." Tom took her hand and guided her up the half-dozen covered steps.

Martha skillfully ascended the throne and sat down with her legs crossed at the ankles, as she had probably learned, Alison was sure, at that Mrs. America contest she was a finalist for in Illinois before they moved here.

"Hi, Alison!" Martha smiled and waved. "Isn't it just too wonderful what these guys are doing?"

"Entirely too wonderful," replied Alison. "We are quite unworthy."

Martha laughed. "Wrong! We are quite worthy. All of us."

Serene. Cheerful. Lovely. That was Martha.

Alison had seen Martha impatient a few times, but never the shrieking maniac that once in a while Alison became. Now and then Alison heard herself say a "damn" or a "hell," something Martha would never, never do.

Alison would never forget the time a storm had left them with a power outage for close to twelve hours. Frustrated at finding her one candle burned down to a stub, she had gone over to Martha's to try to borrow another, leaving Jamie and Melissa grumbling alone with no television or stereo. There were all the Harris children, each with his or her own emergency flashlight, retrieved from the magnetized holder on the left side of their beds, the older two playing their guitars and singing and the younger two dancing as they created finger puppets on the wall.

"Come on over and play," Martha had coaxed. "Go get the kids and help us eat this entire gallon of ice cream before it dies in the non-freezing freezer."

She did, and they partied for hours.

Upon leaving, Alison had said sincerely, "Boy, Martha, you sure do know how to put on a party. My most creative idea for a game is to choose up sides and take naps!''

Nor would Alison ever forget the first Halloween after they moved into the neighborhood. She had sent Jamie and Melissa out trick-or-treating in the paper masks they had chosen from Kmart, a Frankenstein and a Wonder Woman. Alison had stayed by the door, handing out Tootsie Rolls to the various witches and goblins and hoboes who came by.

When she heard the bagpipes, Alison cautiously opened the door to see—four children, the youngest one three, dancing down the sidewalk, flawlessly dressed in Scottish plaid, kilts and caps and long white socks and soft black shoes, performing perfectly the intricate steps of the Highland fling. And behind them, their mother dressed to match and blowing the bagpipes.

''Wow, you guys,'' Alison said, embarrassed to drop her humble little Tootsie Rolls into those tartan drawstringed bags, ''How did you come up with these incredible costumes?''

"Oh, Mom made them," said Anne proudly.

Martha laughed. "I enjoy sewing. It's a hobby I've had for years."

"Do you make—*all* your children's clothes?"

"Most of them."

"Gosh," said Alison, running her fingers over the bright wool plaid, "*I* don't make all my children's clothes. Sometimes I don't even *wash* them all."

Serene. Cheerful. Lovely. And *always* capable. That was Martha.

Alison had actually come to enjoy exaggerating her incompetence in front of her next-door neighbor. And Martha would listen nonplussed as Alison said with a straight face things like, "Come to your Tupperware party? Oh, I've given up on Tupperware, Martha. It melts in the oven."

Or, "Martha, I've come up with the best idea for a nutritional snack for the kids. I poke a multivitamin in their Twinkies!"

Or, "Martha, I have invented the best creative sandwich—put peanut butter on *after* the jelly!"

Or, "Martha, I have solved the mending problem.

I put it in the closet until the kids outgrow it and then give it to the Good Will!''

Or, ''Martha, I've come up with the best idea for getting the children to church on time—put them to bed Saturday night in their Sunday clothes!''

Last December during a lesson at church Martha had said, ''The best thing we can give our children for Christmas is a calm and happy mother.'' Alison had raised her hand and asked, ''Where are they sold?''

No wonder it was Martha and not Alison who was chosen to be Mother of the Year for the Mother's Day program.

''Okay, Martha,'' said Tom, positioning the microphone at center stage, ''here's how it's going to work. After the minister finishes his talk, when we get to the part in the program that says 'Presentation by the Jewels in Our Crown,' you come on out and ascend your throne. Then each of the twenty-six kids comes out in turn carrying a banner with their quote on it, some great statement about mothers. They attach it to one of these little hooks on your throne, see, and then to one of the hooks that go all the way around the crown back there. We've got little steps, see, to help them reach.

"They read their statement, give their one-minute tribute to their own mother, the mother comes up and gets a hug, then they line up behind you right there. By the end of the program we've got twenty-six golden rays going out from your throne to the tips of the crown. Beau-ti-ful!

"Then you step right down here to the microphone and give your 'response.' " Tom extended a hand and helped Martha down from her throne. "And then— ta-da, the big finale—all the kids come forward and sing—"

And here Tom Howard burst into song. "—'M is for the Many things she gave me. . . . ' "

Martha's bright soprano voice joined in. " 'O means only that she's growing Old.' "

"Old?" Martha resonated into the microphone. "Wrong. We are not growing old, are we, Alison? We are eternally young and ever so beautiful."

"Well," said Alison, "some of us are, anyway."

Tom adjusted the mike. "Great song. It's an oldie, but what a goodie! There won't be a dry eye in the house. Then you lead the parade down the stairs here, and everybody follows you out for refreshments. Okay, Martha? Got it?''

''Got it!'' Martha flowed toward stage left and disappeared.

Alison rose and was turning to leave when she heard her daughter's voice behind her. ''Mom!''

Melissa jumped down from the stage and ran to her mother. ''Oh, Mom, I'm glad you haven't gone yet. Jamie and I left our parts in that blue folder in the backseat. Can you bring it in? We're rehearsing downstairs.''

''Sure.''

''Good.'' Melissa leaped back up onto the stage.

''You're welcome,'' Alison called out after her.

''Yeah. Thanks.''

Alison scooted into the backseat of her ten-year-old Toyota and picked up a blue folder, ''Queen of Our Home'' written on the front. She opened it. A couple of pages of instructions. Then a page that was hand-marked ''Jamie Andrews'' over a statement: ''All that I am or ever hope to be I owe to my angel mother—

Abraham Lincoln.'' Alison leaned back on the warm leather and sighed. Angel mother. What a joke.

She cautiously turned the next page and read ''Melissa Andrews'' over a statement: ''God could not be everywhere, so He made mothers.''

Alison closed her eyes and soon felt the little warm drops squeezing out between her eyelids. So He made mothers. Oh, how she would love to be a little piece of God for her children. Even with all their insensitivity and their problems, they were precious, precious beings.

She had never forgotten her face the first time she looked in the mirror after giving birth. It was subtle, but there was something different, something triumphant, something glowing. She had just done something so profound she would never find words for it. She had given life.

And she watched those two lives move and grow and stretch and delight and disappoint and outrage and thrill and break her heart. But always, always it was a miracle and she loved them dearly. They deserved so much. Certainly they deserved a better mother than they were getting in her.

This whole thing was a farce. She was not an angel mother and they were not grateful children. It was all a show, just a painted-on, glitter-glued show to give lip service to the idea of Mother's Day.

Well, there was nothing to do but to play the game. At least her children were here. At least they would have to listen to twenty-six lofty statements about mothers. At least they were willing to stand up there on the stage and give a one-minute tribute to their own mother. At least that was something. They were willing.

Alison picked up the blue folder and headed back to the church.

Chapter
Four

AS SHE WALKED DOWNSTAIRS TO THE BASE-
ment, Alison heard general chaos coming from the rehearsal room. Then at the back by the door the voices
of some of the boys horsing around. She stopped as an
overdramatic voice sang, "M—is for the Mess this stupid program is." That was Brian.

The others laughed.

"O—is for the Obnoxious song we have to sing.
Yeah!" That was Kevin.

More laughter.

"T—is for the Time we're wasting on a good Saturday." Larry.

"Come on, it's not that bad." That was John Harris.

"Boo, boo!"

"H—is for the Helluva stupid program this stupid program is." That was Jamie, her Jamie.

"E—is for Everything dumb this dumb program is." Larry again.

"R—is for the Retarded Reject this stupid program is." Kevin again.

Then Jamie's voice once more. "Put them all together they spell 'Mo-th-er'—the reason we're doing this stupid dumb program in the first place."

Applause and laughter.

"Hey, come on." John Harris again. "You don't have to be here, you know."

"Ohhhhhh, yes we do!" Brian again.

And then Jamie's voice again. "I'd sing ten stupid songs to get to spend a weekend at Cassidy Ranch, everything free including food. Mr. Howard said you could only go if you did the whole bit and got your mother to the program, too."

Alison felt like she'd been kicked in the stomach. So that was it. They were bribed. Tom Howard's father owned a dude ranch and she knew the kids from the church were invited to spend next weekend there for a two-day ride and campout. The kids had talked of hardly anything else for weeks. But she didn't know they had to earn their ticket by being in the program. She didn't know it was a bribe!

Jamie went on. "He had to practically get on his knees to my little sister and then promise her she could have her pick of the horses."

Alison turned away and closed her eyes as someone passed her in the hall.

"Alison? Are you okay?"

"Oh, sure. I'm just—rushed. Could you take this folder in and give it to one of my kids? They forgot it, you know how kids are. I'm—sort of rushed."

"Of course."

And that was the third—and final—straw. It tee-tered on the camel's back of her eternal maternal de-votion all the way home. And then—just as she entered the house—the weight of it settled and the back broke.

She heard it.

She felt it.

Crack!

Alison slammed the door behind her, hard, hard, so hard she heard the glass rattle, and threw two wet swimming suits onto the kitchen floor. She kicked a chair, sending it sprawling halfway across the room. Then she just stood there, arms wrapped tightly around herself, and cried.

Why did I do it? she asked herself. Why did I become a mother? I should have gone off and joined the Peace Corps like I wanted to and done something I'd be appreciated for. Stupid, stupid woman, thinking I could make a contribution to the world by becoming a mother. Stupid, stupid woman! I wish it weren't too late. I wish I could go off and . . .

And this is when the thought first occurred to her. . . . And run away. Just run away. Of course she couldn't run away completely. She couldn't go and join the Peace Corps or anything like that. She had gotten herself into this motherhood thing and she was in it for the long haul.

But she could run away for—a day! She didn't have to face the humiliation of Mother's Day tomorrow! She didn't have to wake up without breakfast in bed and then go to the church program and listen to her children say these outrageously idealistic platitudes that they didn't mean for one minute and sing a song they thought was stupid and in front of everybody give a one-minute tribute to the mother that they did not appreciate at all just so they could spend a weekend at a horse ranch. She didn't have to put up with that!

The kids would be just fine without her for two nights. They had been when she'd had to go to be with her mother for the surgery. And, if anything came up, there was always 911. And a perfect neighbor. Sometimes it came in handy to have a perfect neighbor.

Alison stepped over the wet swimming suits and headed into her bedroom. Yes—that's how she would celebrate Mother's Day this year!

She would run away from home!

Chapter

Five

THROWING A T-SHIRT AND JEANS AND SWEATS into a duffle bag, Alison made a quick plan. Let's see. She could take the pup tent and go up the canyon to Mirror Lake, just a two-hour drive. There were hamburger patties in the freezer. She would serve herself breakfast in sleeping bag and then go for a long hike and then come back and read a book and . . . Or . . .

A light bulb went on behind her eyes and her face lit up.

Holding her breath, Alison ran to the desk drawer and pulled out a coupon she had won at a raffle at the school and thought she would never use. Camping was not good enough for this particular occasion. This was Mother's Day and she was a very, very special mother. So she wasn't a perfect mother. So she wasn't Martha Harris. So what? She was doing a pretty good job without any help, thank you, and she deserved a very, very special Mother's Day. She deserved . . .

There it was. "Fifty percent discount for two nights. The Delphi Hotel." She had only seen this ritzy Greek-themed hotel from the outside but had heard that it was fabulous.

Quickly Alison read the fine print. Last month she had taken the kids out for a free Mexican dinner only to learn the coupon had expired the week before. If she'd been a better mother . . . Oh, forget it.

Good, this coupon was still valid. The room would be somewhere in the neighborhood of one hundred and twenty-five dollars, so she'd actually get two days for the price of one. And she could take enough food with her for tonight and tomorrow.

No! No, she could not. No, she *would* not. This was a very, very special Mother's Day and she was going to eat breakfast in bed. Room service would serve her breakfast in bed, anything she wanted from a big plastic menu. And all this would be paid for—out of their Disneyland money!

Giggling, Alison ran to her chest of drawers and opened the third drawer on the left and reached way to the back behind her winter sweaters and brought out a manila envelope. Four hundred dollars. She would take half, probably not use it all, but it would be good to know she had it if she wanted it.

And then she took the duffle bag and dumped out the sweats and T-shirt and jeans. That was not good enough for a sensational, beautiful, stunning mother like her. She looked best in—hmmmm, that burgundy dress that was just right with the little pearl necklace. She didn't wear that dress nearly enough. It just hung there in the closet waiting, waiting like a wallflower at a dance. Yes, she would like to walk into the Delphi Hotel wearing her burgundy dress and little pearl necklace.

Alison lifted the lid on the rose-colored ceramic heart-shaped container she used for keeping jewelry in. Melissa had made it four years ago in Brownie's and given it to her for Mother's Day. On the underside of the lid there was written in uneven print, "I Love You,

Mom, from Melissa.'' Alison liked to lift the lid and read that. It always made her smile, even though she knew the Brownie leader had made the girls scratch ''I Love You, Mom'' with a toothpick in the wet clay. Melissa had been so proud of making it and baking it and had given it to her with a kiss.

Sometimes Alison would come in and pick up the lid and read it, even when she didn't need jewelry. And it helped. Reading ''I Love You, Mom'' helped, even if it was four years old.

Alison dressed carefully, made it a ritual. Put on makeup. She never wore makeup on Saturday, but this was a special Saturday. A little mascara and her eyes were very, very nice. A bit weary, perhaps, but nice.

And for tomorrow—her Keds and navy slacks and paisley shirt in her best summer colors, in case she wanted to take a walk. But for her hours lounging in the hotel—of course!—that light blue velour lounging outfit that her mother had sent for Christmas and she'd only worn once or twice because she wanted to keep it nice.

Her mother. Guiltily Alison glanced at the photograph on the wall. It was the only picture she had of her mother that she really liked. She looked sincerely happy in that picture. Her long brown hair was piled on her head in big curls and she was wearing that flowered blouse with the big sleeves. Alison had always liked that blouse. In most family pictures her mother looked just a bit pained, or seemed to be trying a little too hard to look pleasant. But in the picture Alison had chosen to put in the good oak frame that hung now on the wall, her mother smiled and looked really quite beautiful.

What would her mother think about this, about her daughter running out on her children for Mother's Day? *She* would never have done it. *She* would have sooner died than abandon her post, no matter how many bombs and bullets were aimed at her.

Oh, it wasn't that bad. But . . . Alison had often looked back on her growing up with regrets. If only she'd been a better daughter . . . Oh, great. More guilt. She remembered sometimes seeing her mother crying, and she knew that it had to be her fault, hers and her two sisters.

Alison threw the lounging outfit into the small suitcase on the bed. "I *wish* Mama would have run away from home," she said out loud. "I *wish* she would have stood up for herself once or twice instead of just crying all the time.'' She slammed the suitcase shut and stood eye to eye with her mother on the wall. ''Well, I'm not going to sit down and cry, Mama. I am out of here!''

Her mother continued to smile.

Alison hurried to her bookshelf. Something to read. Nothing too serious. Nothing too educational. *A Woman of Independent Means.* Yes, the novel she had started and loved and put away because she just couldn't find time to finish it. A perfect book to read in her blue lounging outfit in her room at the Delphi Hotel on Mother's Day.

And now the note to her children.

''Dear Jamie and Melissa—''

She wadded up the piece of yellow scratch paper she'd picked up from the little stack by the telephone. This was not an occasion for an old yellow piece of scratch paper and a pencil. This was an important event and the news deserved to be delivered on the best.

Alison hurried to the desk and rummaged for that box of stationery that had been there forever, the white sheets with the linen-like weave and the gold on the edges like pages of the Bible. Perfect. And a pen that made even, clear, black strokes. Pencils would fade over time and this could be a historical document. Two hundred years from now this could show up in a museum.

"Dear Jamie and Melissa," Alison wrote on the beautiful white paper with clear, black ink strokes. "I am running away from home. But I will be back. I intend to celebrate Mother's Day and appreciate myself. It will be the first bit of appreciation I have felt for some time. There is plenty of food in the refrigerator and in the pantry. Try to finish off the tuna casserole. If you add a little water before heating it, it won't be so dry. I love you both very much. Mother."

She taped the note to the television screen where they wouldn't miss it. Then she grabbed the pen and wrote, "P.S. Do *not* eat the crêpes in the fridge— those are the round things on the pink plate. They are not for you!"

What else? Oh, yes. She quickly dialed a telephone number. "Joan? Hi. Alison. I need to ask you a favor. Could you possibly drop my kids off here when you pick up yours from the rehearsal at church? Something's come up and I'm—I'm not going to be here. Great. Thanks much. I owe you.''

She was set. Money in wallet. Suitcase in hand. Coupon in purse. Oh, oh. What if—

Quickly she pulled the coupon from her purse and dialed the number of the hotel. What if they had no rooms? What if lots of mothers had the same idea? What if she got to the Delphi and there were lines and lines of mothers, young and old, suitcases in hand and weariness in their beautiful mothers' eyes?

''Delphi Hotel. How may I help you?'' The voice was deep and elegant.

''Yes. Do you have a room available for tonight and tomorrow night?''

''We do.''

''Oh, good. Alison Andrews. For one. Just—one.''

On her way out the door, Alison paused, then hurried to the refrigerator, stepping over the wet swimming suits, took a can of orange juice out of the freezer and placed it next to the milk to thaw.

Then she picked up her suitcase and closed the door firmly behind her.

Chapter
Six

ALISON DROVE HALF A BLOCK AND THEN stopped. She put the car in reverse and then put on the brake—not in front of her own house, but in front of Martha's.

"I forgot something," she said to the suitcase sitting patiently in the passenger seat. "Be right back."

Alison got out of the car and walked to the side of the big two-story white house with its perfect lawns and flower beds. "I deserve a rose," she continued, "one of Martha's special, special Mother's Day roses from her special, special Mother's Day rosebushes."

It was not stealing. More than once every season,

Martha would show up at Alison's door with an armful of homegrown roses. "Please," she would say, "take them, take them. They're overgrowing my garden, we have so many."

And Alison would graciously thank her, and place them in the crystal vase she and Gary had gotten as a wedding present and put it on her bedstand so she could go to sleep and wake up to the scent of roses.

And always, as Martha left, she would say, "Please come and get some anytime. I wish you would."

Alison would thank her, and even though she knew Martha was sincere, she never went over and got some roses from her garden. You just don't do that.

But today she did. Today she needed a rose and she knew Martha would be thrilled to give her one, thrilled to give her—yes, that absolutely perfect deep red one right there. Alison twisted the stem until it broke and then wrapped the end in some wet leaves to keep it fresh in the car.

Standing at the reservation desk of the Delphi Hotel, Alison surveyed the lobby. Good thick red and blue carpet. Marble Ionic columns. Gold-leafed chandeliers.

Thinly striped overstuffed chairs. Huge bowls of silk flowers on cherrywood tables. What a good idea this was!

And where were the other women? Where were the long lines of battle-weary mothers with their suitcases in hand? Looked like she was the only one, the only one smart enough to run away from home on Mother's Day.

''Welcome to the Delphi Hotel! May I help you?'' Another deep and elegant voice. A beaming smile. A moustache.

''Yes. Andrews. I called just a bit ago.'' Quickly Alison pulled the coupon out of her purse. ''And I have—this. It's not expired yet.''

''Ah, yes. For one?'' The desk clerk looked at her, Alison thought, a bit suspiciously.

''Yes, one.''

Oh, my word, she thought, he thinks I'm meeting somebody. Here I am in my burgundy dress and pearl necklace asking for a room for one and he thinks I'm meeting somebody. She blushed, then smiled. Well, I am. I'm meeting *me!*

''Oh, and please make a note that under no circumstance am I to be disturbed. No phone calls. Nothing.''

Alison wasn't sure why she said that. Nobody was going to disturb her. Nobody could possibly know she was here. It just sounded so good to say it. I am not to be disturbed. She could never say that at home. But at the Delphi, yes.

For several minutes Alison sat on the edge of the bed, suitcase at her feet. Now what? She had never run away from home before. She bounced a little on the queen-sized mattress. Good. Not too soft. She slipped off her shoes and pressed her toes into the deep pile of the forest green carpet. The clock read four thirty-four.

Unpacking. Of course. That was next.

Alison unpacked and put Martha's red rose in a glass of water on the table by the bed. Then she sat back down. Four thirty-seven.

Any minute now the kids would be coming home. Any minute now they would walk in the door of a motherless house. Jamie would come in first, yelling, "Mo-om!" Then Melissa would enter, calling something like, "I need hiking boots for next weekend. Mo-om?"

No answer. No mother. Melissa would open the

refrigerator and Jamie would go to turn on the television. Frowning, he would read the note as he walked into the kitchen.

"Mom's gone," he would say.

"Gone where?"

"I don't know. She ran away."

"Ran away? What do you mean?"

"That's what it says here, dummy. She ran away from home."

For only a moment Alison saw the rest of the scene the way she wished it would be played. Melissa would reach for the note with shaking hands. Tears would well up in her eyes as she read the news for herself. "Oh, Jamie," she would say. "It's our fault. We've been so bad!"

"I know." Jamie's voice would be gruff from trying to contain his emotion.

"And now we've lost her! What is Mother's Day without a mother?"

Then both children would break into big sobs and pick up their wet swimming suits and hang them on the shower curtain rod the way she had tried to teach them.

But then Alison replayed the scene the way she was sure it would happen. Melissa would look at the note and then shrug and hand it back to Jamie. Jamie would grunt and toss the note into the "re-cyclable" wastebasket and step on the wet swimming suits and haul the milk out of the fridge. "What's to eat?"

Wait! No, no, no, no, no. Alison had forgotten something. They *would* be upset. Terribly upset!

"What?" Jamie would say upon reading the note. His eyes would bulge and he would stand shaking in the middle of the kitchen. "She can't do this to us! She can't be gone on Mother's Day! What about—what about—the horse ranch!"

"Oh, no!" Melissa would gasp. "If she's not at the Mother's Day program—we can't go! Jamie—we've got to *find her!*"

Well, they would never find her. She was safely hidden away in Room 534 on the fifth floor of the Delphi Hotel and they would never find her and they would suffer and it would serve them right.

"Oh, I am in such a quandary," Alison said to the face in the shining oval mirror of the sparkling pink bathroom. "Do I take my bath first or do I order supper from room service first? How *is* it done? And, oh, I wonder if *really good* mothers fold the toilet paper into a point like that so their children can more easily grasp it? I may have to sneak into Martha Harris' bathroom sometime and find out. Well, I believe for my next number I am going to do a magic act."

Alison waltzed to the bed and picked up the telephone and pressed "8."

"I am going to cause food to appear out of nowhere, just like that!" She snapped the fingers of her other hand.

"Yes. This is Room 534. I'd like supper for one, please. I think—the broiled salmon with pearl onions and wild rice. Oh, and apple pie. Thank you!"

She hung up the telephone and continued cheerily speaking. "Well, why do I have to choose? I do believe I will have supper and a bath together, for this is a very special occasion, though I may faint from sensory overload."

*   *   *

"Bubbles—bubbles—many, many bubbles in the bathtub!" sang Alison in her underwear, creating her own melody and emptying the little bottle into the foaming water. If ever she stayed in a motel she brought all the toiletries home to her kids. And at home she would serve herself the smallest piece of pie.

But not today! No, siree! This treat was long overdue and she was going to enjoy every minute of it. "Bubbles and broiled salmon! Broiled, broiled salmon in the bathtub!"

There was a knock at the door and Alison grabbed the hotel's thick white bathrobe.

Sitting submerged in the glistening bubbles nearly to her shoulders, tray balanced carefully across the tub in front of her, Alison smiled a wicked, contented smile. No question, this could become an annual tradition. Around Christmastime the women at church had a session of sharing traditions that strengthened the family. Alison couldn't wait to share this one.

"And now, you sweet thing you, let me turn down the bed for you. Just climb right in in your ever-so-sexy nightgown. Pillows, pillows. Here's your book. Glass of water. Remote control. Now I'm going to give you a massage with *all* of the lotion in this sweet little bottle. And as soon as you're tired, I will sing you a lullaby. Every mother needs a mother to sing her a lullaby."

Eleven fourteen.

The book was on the nightstand. The remote control had clicked off the *Late Show*. The light was on dim. The pillows held a very tired head whose eyes would not stay open.

"You came from a land where all is light
    To a world half day, a world half night.
    To guide you by day you have my love
    And to guard you by night
    Your friends above.
    So sleep, sleep 'til the darkness ends
    Guarded by your angel friends.

Yes, sleep, sleep 'til the darkness ends
Guarded by your angel friends.''

That was the song her mother used to sing to her, the song she sang to her little ones while she was nursing them to sleep. It was a miraculous thing to hold a little baby to your breast. It was a miraculous thing to be a mother.

Alison said her bedtime prayer and envisioned the angels by her bed. And, as always, the angels by the beds of her two children.

One tear fell onto the very soft, very sweet-smelling pillowcase.

Chapter
Seven

ALISON WOKE UP READY TO CELEBRATE. SHE had had a dream in which she stood before the Mother's Bar of Judgment, surrounded by piles of banana bread with a crack down the middle. Dozens of angels pointed their glowing fingers at her sadly and said, "Bad Mother, Bad Mother," and she was led off to where all bad mothers go. But then her cracked banana breads burst open and began to sing and the angels ate of them and were amazed and crowned her "Good Mother" and she sat atop a huge throne with a cosmic display of shooting stars behind it, and then hundreds of grateful children sang and danced at her feet as she joyfully threw them bits of superior banana bread and juicy pieces of broiled salmon.

Alison reached for the phone and pressed "8." She had spent a long time last night determining exactly what this special meal was going to be.

"I am ready for my breakfast in bed now," she purred to room service. "Two pancakes, maple syrup and lots of butter, one egg over easy, hash browns, bacon *and* sausage, cornbread *and* muffin, large orange juice *and* milk. Thank you!"

The children would be having Rice Crispies for breakfast—*if* the milk had not been left out overnight. Martha Harris would be having crêpes and strawberries and vanilla pudding—*if* the Andrews children had not eaten them. But *Alison* would be having *everything!*

She snuggled back into the pillows for another few minutes. Bacon. She knew that bacon was number one on the list of Absolute Worst Foods, and she never served it at home, but—today was special. She was queen—Queen of Our Hotel Room!

"Now, how does that wonderful song go?" Alison sang out in her best shower voice. " 'M' is for the

Magnificent mother that I am. 'O' is for the Ovaries
that I used. 'T' is for the Tough time that I've had and
endured so remarkably well. 'H' is for my Heart so
huge and giving. 'E' is for just Everything great that I
am. 'R' is for the Rest of the terrific things I am. Put
them all together, they spell—'MO-TH-ER,' a word
that means the world to *me!*''

Before she devoured her breakfast with queenly rel-
ish, Alison took out of her wallet some pictures of the
children and propped them up by the lamp. So many
emotions filled her, all stirred up together in a strange
motherly soup. She was peeved at them but loved them
and was having a wonderful time without them but
missed them.

That picture with nine-year-old Jamie and the string
of fish always made her smile. After numerous pitiful
attempts at taking her son fishing, always coming away
from the river with empty hands and a little more guilt,
Alison had the bright idea of taking him to a fish farm,
where they guaranteed a catch. Just look at that grin!

How had she lost him? If she would have ever asked

him that, he would have just grunted and said, "I'm still here." But he wasn't there really, not for her, and it broke her heart.

When Jamie was small he was her sweetheart man, her little shadow, and he would laugh and laugh as she put Cheerios and bits of apple between her teeth and fed him like a baby bird.

Even into elementary school he was still her darling. She met him coming home from first grade one day and he said, "Mom, I know why God sends babies to mothers."

"Why?" she had asked.

"Because if they didn't go to mothers they would land on the sidewalk and go splat! They need something soft to land on."

Alison had thought about that a lot. How to be soft—but not so soft you get stepped on. How to be a mother that mothers instead of smothers. How to do your job so well that finally you do yourself out of a job. How to be a mother to a boy who was not yet a man. How to do the hardest job in the entire world.

The tension that had grown between Alison and her oldest child was palpable. It wasn't that he made choices without any regard for what his mother thought. Sometimes Alison felt he gave careful attention to what his mother thought—and then did just the opposite. His choices of clothing—hair style—music—leisure time—grammar. Did he *have* to say, "Me and Dave went . . . ?" He knew better than that. It bugged her. *Everything* he did seemed to bug her. Everything he did seemed done in *order* to bug her.

And everything she did seemed to bug him. Just the other day she had been singing an old Judy Garland number to herself in the kitchen. And Jamie had said, "Mo-om, when my friends get here, would you please not sing? It is so embarrassing and you only know stuff that's fifty years old."

By the time she turned to look at him, he had left the room, and she wasn't sure if he had seen the tears in her eyes he'd have even cared. There were actually quite a few times she'd had tears in her eyes over her oldest child. He had no use for her now—except for food and transportation and new jeans and his weekly allowance. Her mind, her heart—he had no interest in those. Whatever influence she used to have was long gone.

And Melissa—she wasn't quite a teenager yet, not in body anyway. But she was slipping away just the same.

Look at that picture, that great picture Alison had shot of Melissa in her ballet outfit. So long ago, those days when her daughter cared more than anything that her *mother* was in the audience at the recital, that her *mother* watched as she did her flips in gymnastics, that her *mother* tucked her in bed and sang her a lullaby.

"I love you big as the whole world and out to the stars," Melissa used to say. And she would come to her mother for an answer to every question—like why the water in the bathtub is not blue like the water in the lake—because she was certain her mother knew absolutely everything there was to know.

But these days Melissa was frequently snippy with her mother, and would sigh indulgently if she expressed an opinion, and hadn't initiated an "I love you" for a long time.

Mother's Day Sunday continued as a perfect day of rest. Usually Alison's idea of a day of rest was to do everything you can Monday through Saturday and the rest on Sunday. But not today!

And then the telephone rang.

Alison let it ring three times. Nobody could possibly be calling her. Maybe room service wanted to tell her of the specials that evening.

"Hello?"

The very deep voice answered. "Ms. Andrews?"

"Yes."

"This is the front desk. I know you left instructions, but we have someone here who wishes to see you. May we give them your room number?"

"No!" Alison fairly shouted the word.

"Very well. We always try to ensure the privacy of our guests. I will tell them no."

"Are there two of them?"

"Yes."

"A boy and a girl?"

"Yes."

"Are they bleeding?"

A pause. "No, they don't seem to be."

"Ask them if the house is on fire."

A pause, about as long as it takes for someone to roll his eyes. "She wants to know if the house is on fire." Another pause. "No, Ma'am, they tell me the house is not on fire."

"Then tell them to go home!"

"She says to go home."

"Mo-om!" That was Melissa in the background.

"You've got to come to the church—" That was Jamie.

Alison slammed down the telephone. How in the world did they find her? This was incredible. She ran away from home and did it absolutely perfectly, and now here they were right on her doorstep.

The phone rang again. She picked it up and said nothing.

"Ma'am? Ma'am? The children say they really must talk to you. You *are* their mother?"

"Yes, I am their mother, and the only reason they want to talk to me is that it's Mother's Day and they want to go to the horse ranch! And that's not a good enough reason! And I'm staying away from home all day long, and I have only one question for them. How did they find me?"

A long sigh. "She wants to know how you found her."

"We pushed the redial, like I saw them do in a detective show. This was the last number called on our phone." The voice was Melissa's.

"Ma'am? She says they pushed—oh, this is getting ridiculous. . . ."

"I heard her! Tell them they are very clever, but they are also very insensitive and selfish to use me like this and they can just go home!"

Alison slammed the phone down again. How *dare* they!

She walked to the window, pulled back the drapes, and looked down. Two bicycles, a blue one and a red one, right there chained to the flagpole. The Delphi Hotel was too ritzy for a bicycle rack.

A prisoner, that's what she was now! She had bounded for freedom and here she was a prisoner, a prisoner of war!

She had been planning to go down and browse in the hotel's gift shop and maybe even buy a postcard or two or even something like a little crystal paperweight to commemorate this great and grand day. She was going to change out of her powder blue lounging suit into her navy slacks and paisley shirt and go outside and take a walk in the hotel's famous rose garden, which the brochure on her desk said had one hundred and eighty varieties from all over the world.

And then she was going to change out of her slacks and shirt back into her burgundy dress with her pearl necklace and go down to the dining room with its elegant china and its crystal chandeliers and have chateaubriand for one. And now they had ruined it all. She couldn't set foot outside her door.

She was a prisoner!

Oh, well. The novel was getting really good. Alison plumped the pillows back up on the bed and opened the book.

Chapter
Eight

THIRTY PAGES LATER A KNOCK SOUNDED AT the door. "Maid service!" The voice was high and cheerful.

Alison slowly walked to the door and stared at it suspiciously.

"Maid service!"

Keeping the chain in place, Alison opened the door just a couple of inches, and peered into the hall. Good. It *was* the maid.

Alison shut the door quickly behind the pretty, young Asian woman and locked it again.

"I clean fast," the maid said as she hurried into the bathroom.

Alison arranged her chair so she could watch the maid carefully while she cleaned the bathroom, tidied the bedroom, and made the bed—not to make sure she did it right, certainly, but because Alison found it so fascinating to watch another human being *make her bed!* And wipe *her* sink and bathroom counter, and clean the ring and perhaps a salmon bone or a little pearl onion or two from *her* bathtub, and empty *her* wastebaskets, and pick up the towel from the floor that *she* had left there, and fold the toilet paper to a nice point just for *her!*

Alison had to resist the urge to help the maid make the bed. Beds are so much easier to make with four hands instead of two—all mothers know that. But not today, no siree, no bed-making today!

When she heard running out in the hallway and knocking on doors, Alison was not immediately alarmed. But as the knocking grew louder and closer and she heard, "Mo-m! *Mo-om!*" she knew she was not yet home free. Bam! Bam! Bam! A heavy knock on 536 just next door, and then Jamie's voice. "Mo-om! It's an *emergency!*"

The maid looked up in concern. "My, what is that?"

"I don't hear anything." Alison held her book a little higher.

Bam! Bam! Bam! A pounding on the door just across the hall. "Mo-om! We *need* you!"

"Somebody lost their mother," said the maid as she headed for the door. "Maybe I help them find manager."

"No!" Alison dropped her book and ran past the maid, throwing her body in front of the door. "No! You're—you're not finished making my bed. I—I need my bed—made!"

Looking at Alison strangely, the maid backed up to the bed and hurriedly finished arranging the quilted floral spread.

Bam! Bam! Bam! The pounding and the running footsteps were farther away now. "Mo-om! Please!" Footsteps down a stairwell. Silence.

Then the telephone.

The maid darted a cautious glance at her as Alison picked up the telephone.

"Yes?"

"Madam!" The voice was elegant *and* icy. "Your children are disturbing the guests. They are running up and down the hallways pounding on doors and calling for you!"

"Arrest them!" Alison slammed down the telephone.

The maid looked at her warily and backed her cleaning cart toward the door.

"Happy Mother's Day!" Alison sat down on her newly made bed and smiled. "If you are a mother."

"Yes. I am mother. Two children." She gestured at the pictures Alison had placed by her lamp. "You mother too?"

"Oh, yes!" Alison slapped the very poofy pillow. "Yes, I am definitely a mother!"

"Happy day to you too." And with that the maid hurriedly opened the door and was gone.

Alison chained the door again and sat back down.

Whew! They were not giving up easily, those children of hers. She had tried to teach them perseverance but hadn't seen much evidence that she'd succeeded until now. What would they try next? If she heard the fire alarm—she would definitely, absolutely not budge!

Alison picked up the telephone, punched "9" and then dialed her mother's number. She had sent a card last week, but called every Sunday anyway.

"Mama? Happy Mother's Day!"

"Well, same to you. How you doing?"

"Great. I am having the *best* Mother's Day! Treated like a queen, waited on hand and foot."

"Really?"

"Mama, you know what?"

"What?"

"You are a beautiful woman."

Silence on the other end.

"Mama? I was looking at your picture—you know the one I like with your hair all curly and up—and I thought, 'My mother is a beautiful woman.' "

"Oh, my. What'd *you* have for breakfast?"

"You don't want to know."

"Well, then—thank you."

"I know you don't hear that very often, Mama, but I thought you should. Mama—when we were little, did you sometimes feel, well, like a failure, like we didn't appreciate you at all?"

"Sure. Goes with the territory."

"Hmmm. Well, I'm sorry—for the bad times we gave you. I know it's a little late, but I apologize for—for—being your kid."

Alison's mother laughed, and Alison joined her.

"Well, you could always make me laugh, baby girl. No matter what, you could always make me laugh. I've always been glad you chose me."

"Think I chose you, huh? You mean it's not a crapshoot, what mother gets what kid? Think there's some sense behind it?"

"Oh, yeah. No accidents there. I think every child gets the right mother, the one that's got just the right strengths and the right weaknesses so the right learning can take place. I've forgiven my mother, and you've forgiven your mother."

"And my kids will forgive theirs."

"Yep."

Alison sighed. "But—but how do we forgive our kids?"

Alison's mother laughed again. "Oh, we do. Eventually."

"I love you, Mama."

"I love you too, sweetheart."

"Happy Mother's Day."

"You too."

"And in conclusion, Mama, do you know what Winnie the Pooh and John the Baptist have in common?"

"No. What?"

"They've got the same middle name!"

Alison's mother was still laughing when they hung up.

Twenty pages further into the book, Alison stood up and stretched. She really would love to go for a walk in the rose garden and get a little air. Moving to the window, Alison pulled back the thin white curtain and looked down.

No bicycles at the flagpole.

Good. They had given up and gone home.

Chapter Nine

DRESSED IN HER PAISLEY SHIRT AND NAVY slacks, Alison strolled out the east door of the Delphi Hotel into the rose garden. No one was in sight but an elderly couple with translucent skin, holding hands and walking slowly. The combined scent of one hundred and eighty different varieties of roses rolled at her in little waves and she took a deep breath, letting it out in a sigh.

Several marble statues were spaced along the paths that made the rose garden into a lovely labyrinth. Alison walked past Zeus with his thunderbolt, then Hades in his chariot, and stopped in front of Demeter, bountiful mother, one hand holding a sheaf of grain and the other lovingly holding the hand of Persephone, the abducted daughter she would not rest until she had found.

''Hi, Demeter.'' Alison raised her hand in salute. ''Happy Mother's Day. This year I'm not chasing after my kids like you did, I'm running from them. Maybe next year.''

She sat on the bench that circled the statue and chose one full yellow brier to appreciate. So soft. So many velvet petals arranged so magically. A little miracle on a stem.

''Mo-om!'' The voice was a high-pitched, grating yell and came from the direction of the swimming pool.

Alison stood up quickly, a thorn scratching her wrist as she did.

''Jamie!'' A louder yell. ''She's over there—in the garden!''

Alison bolted for the east door of the Delphi. She ran past Hades, past Zeus. Just up the three steps and she would be in!

Suddenly her five-foot-ten-inch son was in front of her, blocking the entrance with his arms.

''Mom! Please—!''

Without a word Alison turned and ran down a different path. "Excuse me," she said to the elderly couple with the translucent skin, all the while thinking, What am I doing?—I am running away from a five-foot-ten-inch football player. But she kept on running, past Artemis on her horse, past Poseidon with his trident.

"Mo-om!"

There was her daughter in front of her.

There was her son behind her.

Alison leaped up onto the bench that surrounded the statue of the armored Athena, a shield over her arm and a spear in her hand.

"How dare you?" Fire was in Alison's eye and outrage in her voice as she looked down on them. It felt good to look down on them. "I am a human being! I am your mother! I am not your ticket to the horse ranch!"

Her children stood panting in front of her. Then Jamie spoke urgently. "It's not the horse ranch, Mom."

"It isn't the Mother's Day program at all," Melissa added.

"It's not?" Alison looked suspiciously from one to the other.

"No," said Jamie. "It's *Martha!*"

Alison blinked and shook her head a little. "Martha?"

"I'll tell," Melissa jumped in, then poured out the story as if she were running a marathon. "Martha's locked herself in the bathroom at church and she's crying and crying and she says she's never coming out. Never. And the program's supposed to start in an hour if the Fire Department says people can come in."

"Fire Department?" Alison slowly stepped down and sat on Athena's marble bench.

"We were having one last run-through this morning, and Michael—you know, Martha's ten-year-old—well, Brian and Kevin dared him to throw a firecracker under the throne when his mom sat down on it, and he said no and they called him a Goody Two-shoes, so he said yes, but what they gave him was a whole *pack* of firecrackers and when they went off it was like gunshots—oh, Mom, it was loud!—and Martha screamed and ran. And it knocked over a can of rubber cement that was left open under the throne, so it spilled and caught fire, and in just a second the throne was in flames and all of the streamers with the motherhood stuff caught on fire, and Mr. Howard got the fire extinguisher and we got water from the taps, and then the Fire Department got there with a police officer because someone had called nine-one-one.''

''Oh, Mom,'' Jamie broke in, sitting down beside his mother on the bench, ''Martha was so *mad!* She was yelling at Michael.''

''She was?'' Alison's eyes opened wide.

''And she said some awful bad words, Mom, right there in the church.''

Alison grinned. ''She *did?*''

''And then she started crying and said that no way is she Mother of the Year and she's a bad mother or her son would not have committed vandalism and burned up her throne, and even if they cleaned up the stage she is not going to do her response to the jewels in our crown, and that's when she ran into the ladies' bathroom and locked the door, and she's still in there crying and crying and Mister Howard or anybody can't get her to come out.''

Jamie crouched down on the path in front of his

mother. "Mom, you've got to. You've got to go to the church and bang on the bathroom door and tell Martha she's okay and that she's got to come out and be Mother of the Year. She's not a bad mother, Mom."

Alison smiled. "Well, of course she's not."

"She's a good mother."

"Of course she is. But why me?"

Both children looked at her as if she had asked them why the sun rose.

"Well, because . . ." Jamie shrugged his shoulders and looked at his sister.

"Because—you're—you're our *mom!*" Melissa said earnestly. "You can do *anything!* You're sort of like—like—God—could not be everywhere, and so—" Melissa's voice got soft. "And so—He made—you."

Alison stared at her daughter. She had never seen Melissa's face so open and sincere.

Jamie jumped to his feet. "You're the only one who can do this, Mom, I know you are. You always know the right thing to say."

"I do?"

"Well, sure." Jamie was a little impatient now.

"Like when I scratched you-know-what on the principal's door and you said to me, 'When you choose the very first step on a path, you also choose the last, so if you don't like the end of the road you'd better back up fast'—well, if you hadn't said that I'd probably never have actually apologized to Mr. Adams in person and asked if I could help tutor in the Special Ed room."

Alison drew in a little gasp. "You did?"

Jamie kicked a rock and turned partly away. "I never would have, except for you. Well, anything good I ever did—or probably ever will do . . ."

Alison watched as a blush crept up her son's neck and onto his cheeks.

". . . I—I owe to my—angel mother."

Melissa covered her mouth to stifle a giggle.

Jamie grinned an embarrassed grin and punched his sister's shoulder.

As for the mother, she threw back her head and laughed.

The parking lot was two-thirds full when Alison's Toyota screeched to a stop.

"Hurry!" yelled Melissa, who hit the ground running first. "Seventeen minutes. Just seventeen minutes 'til the program's supposed to start!"

The Andrews family raced in the side door, raced past Tom Howard, who was pacing and praying and gesticulating frantically between heaven and the women's bathroom, raced past the general pandemonium of confused young people in the hallway, and arrived at the locked bathroom door, upon which several of the Harris children were pounding.

"Mom! Mom, I'm sorry I burned up your throne! I didn't mean to!"

"Mom! Come out! Please!"

"Out of the way! Out of the way!" Jamie dispersed the cluster of Harris children and Alison stepped up to the door.

Rapping sharply, she called out, "Martha? Martha, it's the police! Open up!"

"Go away, Alison! Everybody, go away!" The voice behind the bathroom door was mournful.

"You are under arrest for being ridiculous, Martha! There are two hundred people in the hall who love you and more are streaming in every minute. Now, blow your nose and get out here and be Mother of the Year!''

"*You* go be Mother of the Year, Alison. You deserve it more than I do!''

"What?''

Very slowly the bathroom door opened and a hand grasped Alison's wrist and pulled her inside. There the two women stood, face to face.

This was a Martha Alison had never seen. Little moist beads covered her forehead and temples and her white silk blouse was damp and clingy. Alison never knew that Martha perspired. Her Mary Kay makeup was streaked, and black mascara made two dark little rivulets down her cheeks. A pearl comb dangled from wispy strands on one side of her head, and its pearly mate was on the floor. Her pink heels were kicked into the corner by the wastebasket.

Martha slumped onto the closed toilet and drew her feet up, hugging her knees. Little sobs like hiccups punctuated her speech. "I wish—I were more like you, Alison. I've always—envied you.''

"Me?'' Alison glanced at herself in the mirror.

"You know how to—handle things. I don't know how to—handle things. I work and work—and work and work—to make things go perfectly so there'll be nothing—to handle. But when things don't go perfectly—I don't know how to—handle it." Martha began to cry louder and pulled another handful of toilet paper from the roll, pressing it to her nose.

"No kidding?" asked Alison. "I've spent years envying *you!* You like the way I handle stuff?"

"Oh, yeah!" Admiration filled Martha's voice. "You just sort of—go with the flow. You would have never fallen apart like this. You would have made some joke—like—like: 'Boy, that was the biggest whoopie cushion *I've* ever sat on!' "

Alison laughed. "Martha. You just made a joke."

"I did?"

"Say it again, but cross your eyes like this."

Martha burst into a sob-laugh and held the toilet paper over her mouth, shaking.

"But don't say it to me. Say it to your kids. Say it to poor little Michael. And don't forget to cross your eyes. But first, wash your face and fix your hair. Jeez, Martha, you look *awful!*"

Alison ducked and a big wad of toilet paper bounced off the wall behind her. "And now, Martha, I am *really* going to make your day. You know how well I handle things? I handle things so well that yesterday I couldn't handle one more thing and I ran away from home."

Martha gasped in delight. "You did?"

"I did, girlfriend. But I'm back. I'm not down for the count, and neither are you. Come on, Mother of the Year, move it, move it."

Of the three hundred people gathered for the Mother's Day program, nobody enjoyed it more than Alison. She sat in the front row and had a perfect view of Martha Harris as she stood on the hastily constructed pedestal that was covered with gold and white throw rugs. And when the two jewels in Alison's crown came out and said their pieces, she went up for her hug, beaming brighter than the footlights. And she sqeezed each of their hands and chuckled during Martha's excellent "response" when she said, "The road of motherhood is not always smooth, and there are as many ways to be a mother as there are women. But, as someone I admire a lot told me just a few minutes ago, 'Heck, if we can just manage not to eat the kids' chocolate bunnies before Easter, we're doing a pretty good job. *All* of us!' ''

Sure enough, just as Tom Howard had predicted, the audience would not stop applauding and there wasn't a dry eye in the house.

Later that night at the Delphi Hotel, Alison Andrews and her two children celebrated the rest of Mother's Day by ordering from room service baked chicken and garlic potatoes and cheesecake, after which they ate the lemon meringue pie that Melissa had made that morning just in case her mother came home after all and even cleaned up the kitchen by herself.

And it wasn't until two in the morning—even on a night before school—that the slumber party in Room 534 ended and Alison sang a lullaby to her big girl on the other side of the bed and her son already snoring softly on the floor.

That night she dreamed of flowers, all kinds of them, growing and blossoming and perfuming the air. And she noticed for the first time that not only was morning glory lovely, but it was very, very hardy, fast growing, and following a frost came back beautifully year after year after year after year.